BEAR TAKES A TRIP

Written by Stella Blackstone

Illustrated by Debbie Harter

Barefoot Books

Step inside a story

Bear has a very long journey to make.
There are lots of things for him to take.

7:00 am

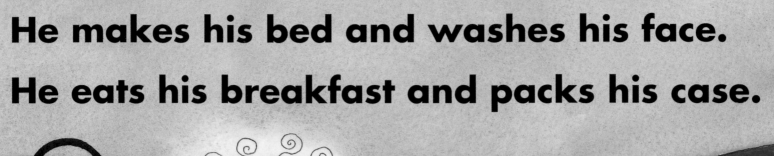

He makes his bed and washes his face.

He eats his breakfast and packs his case.

8:30 am

He hops on the bus at the end of the lane. It takes him through town where he'll get on the train.

9:00 am

He meets his friend, who is coming too.
They chat about everything they want to do.

10:00 am

At the railway station, they have to wait.
The train to the mountains is always late.

10:30 am

Here it comes! The bears find their seats.
They open their picnics and share some treats.

11:15 am

They race out of town and follow the coast.
Bear can't decide which sights he likes most.

12 noon

At long last, the journey comes to an end.
Bear has a cabin and so does his friend.

1:45 pm

The bears learn to sail on a mountain lake.
They also go climbing and they get back late.

4:00 pm

They have lots of fun, whatever the weather.

Bear wants to stay here forever and ever!

5:30 pm

Bear Tells the Time

Can you see the time and spot the clock as Bear enjoys his trip? Help Bear tell the time.

12 o'clock in the middle of the day is called noon. 12 o'clock in the middle of the night is called midnight. Times from midnight to noon are called am. Times from noon to midnight are called pm. The short hand of the clock points to the hour. The long hand of the clock points to the minute.

15 minutes	30 minutes	45 minutes	60 minutes
quarter of an hour	half an hour	three quarters of an hour	one hour

Twenty past one
1:20 pm

One o'clock
1:00 pm

Ten past one
1:10 pm

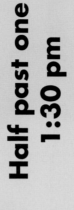

What time is it?

Half past one
1:30 pm

Quarter to two
1:45 pm

Five to two
1:55 pm

For more fun with Bear:

BEAR IN A SQUARE

BEAR ABOUT TOWN

BEAR IN SUNSHINE

BEAR'S BUSY FAMILY

BEAR AT HOME

BEAR'S BIRTHDAY

BEAR ON A BIKE

BEAR AT WORK

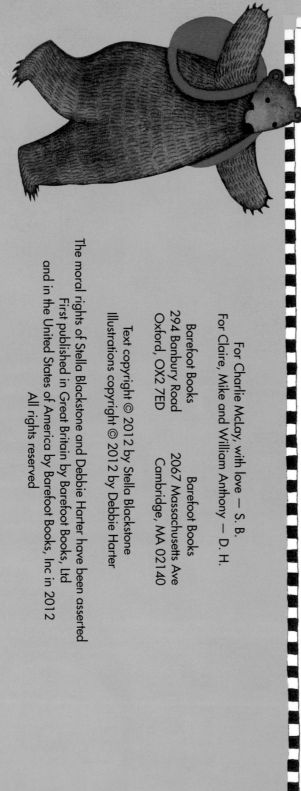

Barefoot Books
294 Banbury Road
Oxford, OX2 7ED

Barefoot Books
2067 Massachusetts Ave
Cambridge, MA 02140

Text copyright © 2012 by Stella Blackstone
Illustrations copyright © 2012 by Debbie Harter

The moral rights of Stella Blackstone and Debbie Harter have been asserted
First published in Great Britain by Barefoot Books, Ltd
and in the United States of America by Barefoot Books, Inc in 2012
All rights reserved

Graphic design by Judy Linard, London
Reproduction by B & P International, Hong Kong
Printed in China on 100% acid-free paper
This book was typeset in Slappy and Futura
The illustrations were prepared in paint, pen and ink, and crayons

British Cataloguing-in-Publication Data:
a catalogue record for this book is available from the British Library
Library of Congress Cataloging-in-Publication Data is available under
LCCN 2011036847

ISBN 978-1-84686-756-9

3 5 7 9 8 6 4 2

For Charlie McLay, with love — S. B.
For Claire, Mike and William Anthony — D. H.